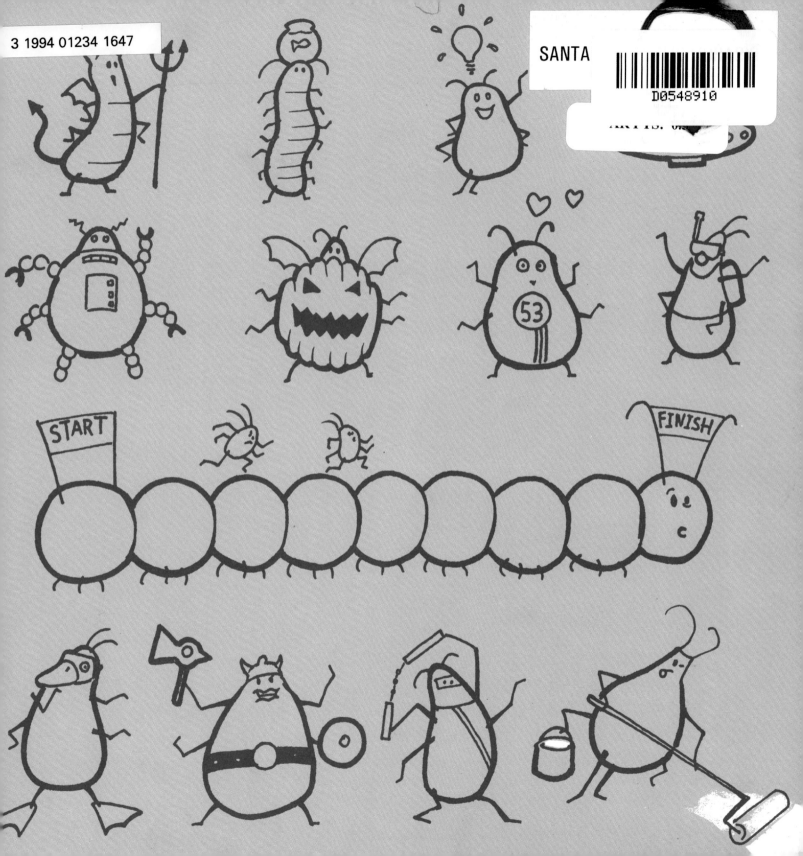

Doorknob the Rabbit
and the Carnival of Bugs

by SerWacki

Tricycle Press
Berkeley/Toronto

To my little pile of perfect friends
and my incredibly functional family.
Special thanks to Abigail, Chris,
Jenny, Ken, Lynn, and Ronnie.

Text and illustrations copyright © 2005
by SerWacki

Tricycle Press
a little division of Ten Speed Press
P.O. Box 7123
Berkeley, California 94707
www.tenspeed.com

Design by Randall Heath
Typeset in Poppl–Laudatio
The illustrations in this book were rendered in
acrylic gouache.

Library of Congress Cataloging-in-Publication Data
SerWacki.
Doorknob the Rabbit and the carnival of bugs /
written and illustrated by SerWacki.
p. cm.
Summary: When Doorknob the Rabbit is unable
to get rid of a houseful of bugs, the reader is
invited to help out.
ISBN 1-58246-143-0
[1. Rabbits--Fiction. 2. Insects--Fiction.] I. Title.
PZ7.S4886Do 2004   [E]--dc22   2004016106

First Tricycle Press printing, 2005
Printed in Singapore

1 2 3 4 5 6 – 09 08 07 06 05

Doorknob the Rabbit had won the Crown Mallard at the 32nd annual Festival of Ducks.

RABBIT WINS CROWN DUCK!

CARNIVAL OF BUGS DRAWS NEAR!

DUCKS FOR BUNNIES

He was finally home and his favorite flower, Sibbly, was very happy to see him. She had a cup of dandelion tea waiting for him, just cool enough to drink.

So with a sip, a yawn, and drooping ears, he put his award on the shelf,

slipped into his favorite pair of stripy sleeping socks,

curled up around Sibbly, and promptly went to sleep with his nose gently wiggling.

Doorknob dreamed sweet dreams of ducks . . . .

until a pounding on the door stopped his dreams from singing and his nose from wiggling.

When Doorknob opened his door, he found six thousand prickly bugs waiting on his front stoop.

"Hello," they announced with wide smiles. "We're going to have our carnival in your rumpus room!"

But I don't have a rumpus room.

As they crawled in, six thousands bugs made footprints on his clean floors

and brought in trumpets, balloons, and banners.

♥ BUGS

There were even some hungry aphids eyeing
Sibbly and licking their greedy chompers.

Doorknob politely pointed out the house guest rules.

HOUSEGUEST RULES
No bugs or elephants
Wipe your feet
No Trumpets after dark
Do not touch my flower

BUT, the spelling bees rewrote every rule . . .

BUGS RULE!
Bee noisy!
Bee messy!
Don't beehave!

Stop calling the moon!
Telephone Book
Australia- 555-555-5555
China- 555-555-5567
The Moon- 555-
Very

Run Sibbly Run!!
M

"That's it!"

Doorknob called Paul's Pest Pounders.
"Paul! There's a Carnival of Bugs in my house and I can't get one nose wiggle of sleep. Can you come over right now?"

"Geez, buddy," said the exterminator, "didn't you read the newspaper? Nobody can stop a Carnival of Bugs."

CLICK!

CARNIVAL OF BUGS CAN'T BE STOPPED!

The situation was looking hopeless, but then Sibbly had an idea which made Doorknob say . . . HMMMMMMMMMM

Doorknob played his flute, hoping to lure the bugs away.

Out the door and down the street he skipped.

Not one bug followed him out . . .

but hordes of giggling mice followed him back . . .

and they wouldn't leave because The Beetles were playing.

"Hungry cats should do the trick," said Doorknob.

So he hopped onto the computer and placed an order with catsinaminute.com.

CatsInaMinute.com

Quantity: ALL

One minute later the cats arrived.

HI

They were the most famous troupe of magician cats in the WORLD.

And they made Doorknob the star of their most famous trick.
Everyone asked to see it again . . . and **again** . . . and **AGAIN!**

So, faced with six thousand prickly bugs, a horde of
giggling mice, and dozens of magic cats all trying to
pull him out of their top hats, one really couldn't
blame a bunny for what he did next.

"HOORAY!" cheered the bugs. "Now we can have our boat race!"

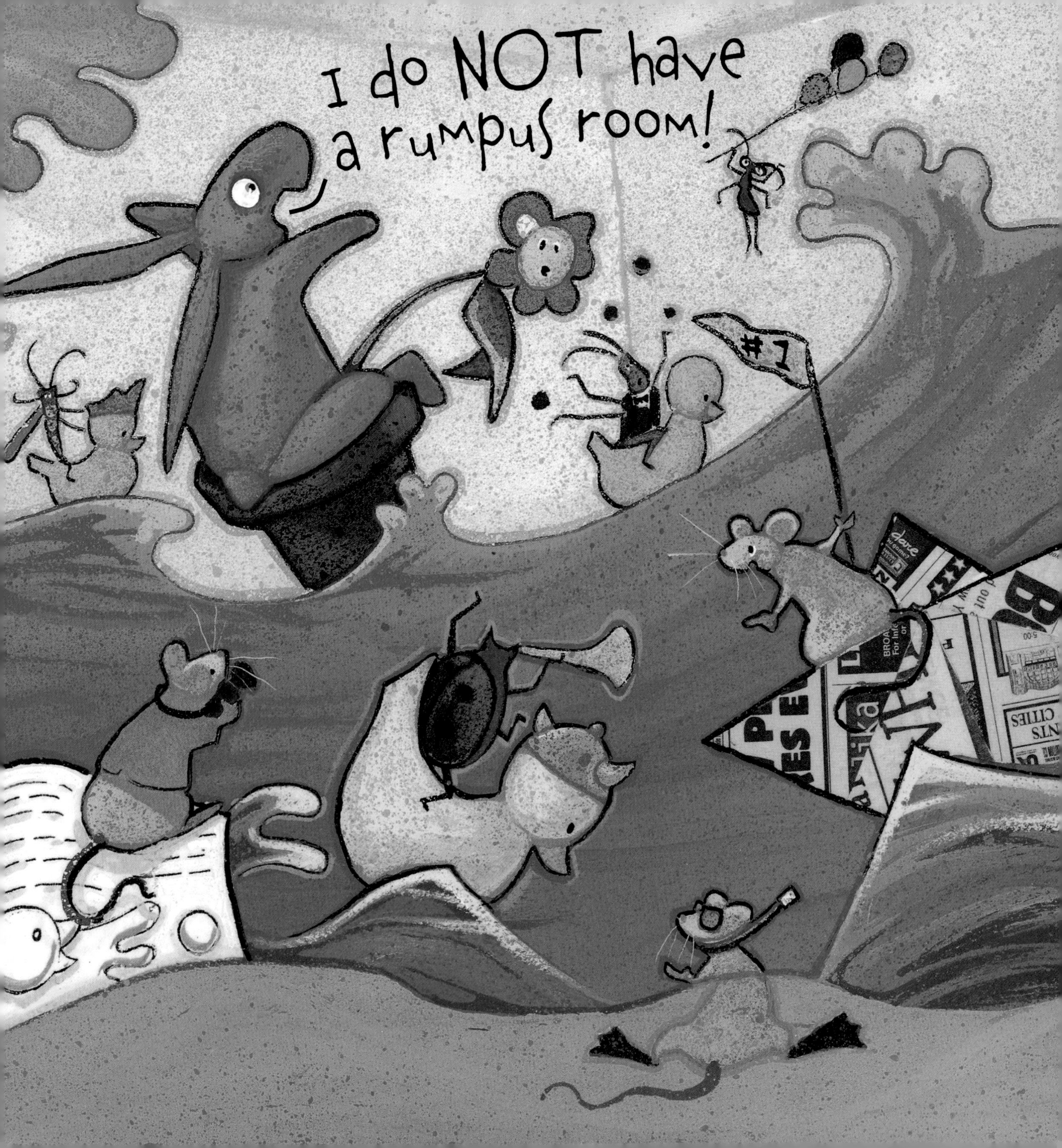
I do NOT have a rumpus room!

It was true, Doorknob didn't have a rumpus room. He had a whole rumpus house!

Even the gentlest and sweetest of rabbits has a cork that can pop. Doorknob's was blasted into outer space.

POP

lapin bleu fâché

What could he do to stop the Carnival of Bugs? He had tried rules, he had tried calling for help, he had tried luring them with music, he had even tried flooding them out.

But, there **IS** one thing that can stop a Carnival of Bugs.

YOU. You can close this book.

If you really want to help me you will slam this book shut RIGHT NOW!

Oh!

Of course Doorknob forgot that he was in the book, too.

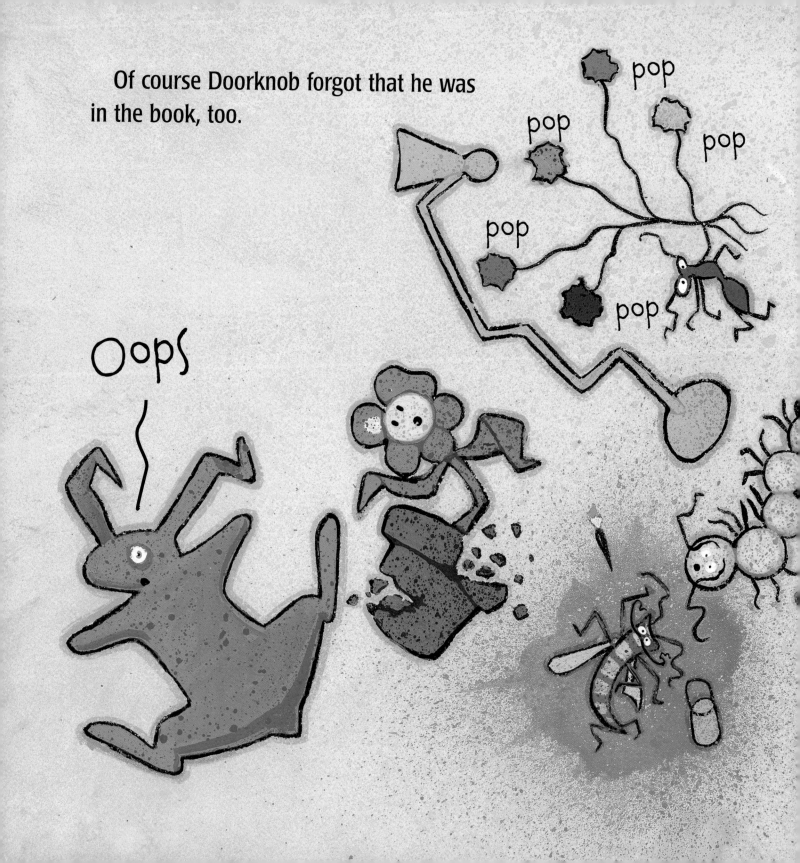

It worked! The bugs set off for somewhere less squishable,
and Doorknob and Sibbly were left in peace at last.

KNOCK!
KNOCK!
KNOCK!

Until there came another knocking.

But Doorknob was no dumb bunny.

He didn't even open the door.

THE END

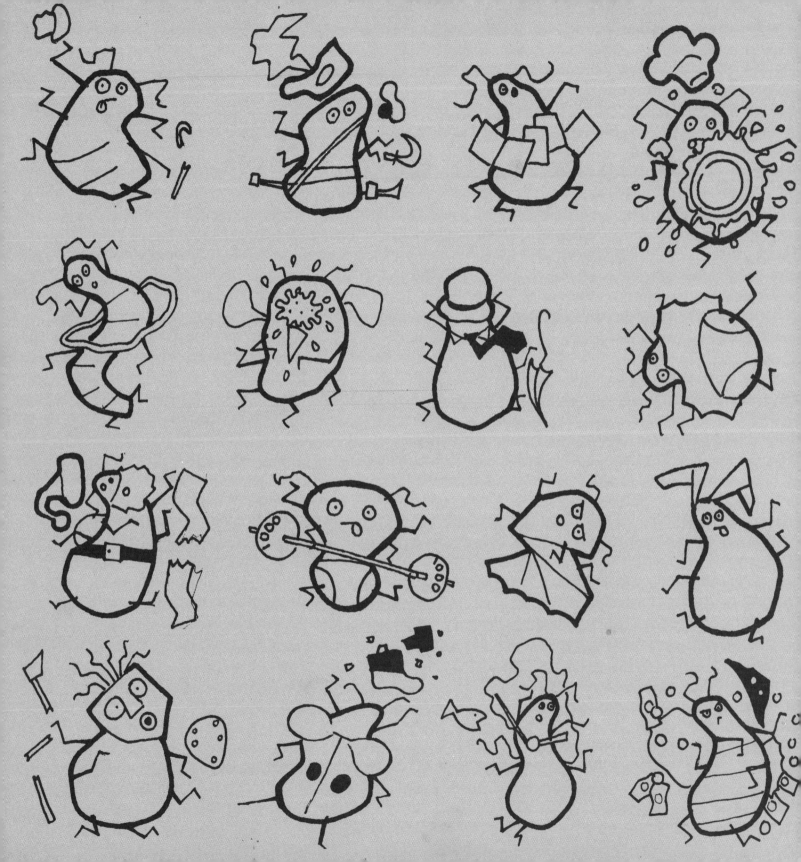